BARMI

Barmi is a fictional city. This pre-Roman settlement that grew to become a major twentieth-century metropolitan area cannot be located on any map. Its name does not appear in the pages of almanacs or history books. It could exist, however, almost anywhere in the Mediterranean coastal zone that stretches from the mouth of Spain's Ebro River to that of Italy's Tiber River.

The layout of Barmi's streets, the history of its fortified walls, and the splendor of its public buildings and monuments mirror the authentic southern European cities whose sagas – dating from the fourth century B.C. to the present – inspired the drawings, diagrams, and text of this book. A shared cultural history binds all these cities. In them, Latin influences are as pronounced as Western European ones. Their histories include phases of tribal settlement, Roman colonization, feudalism, and, more recently, massive industrialization. The wealth of their cultural and artistic achievements is in part a reflection of the Mediterranean region's mild, nurturing climate.

The Roman conquerors of Mediterranean Europe's pre-Christian tribes managed to fuse the legacies of a thousand older societies into a single spirit. The cultures that followed contributed new religions, technology, and attitudes, which combined with existing institutions to create rich, new syntheses. Here, "civilization" assumed the face we recognize today.

Barmi is a composite of these southern European cities, to which Western civilization owes so much. They have witnessed centuries of creative endeavor and humanistic advances. Their buildings and squares are the ancient stages on which great events were played out. Their streets – the scene of centuries of political struggle and social upheavals – still echo with the clamor of those long-ago, and not so long-ago, events.

BARMI

A MEDITERRANEAN CITY THROUGH THE AGES

XAVIER HERNANDEZ • PILAR COMES

Illustrated by
JORDI BALLONGA

Translated by Kathleen Leverich

Houghton Mifflin Company
Boston 1990

1. FARMERS AND HERDERS: 4th Century B.C.

1. FARMERS AND HERDERS
4TH CENTURY B.C.

In the fourth century B.C. a small fortified town grew up on a hill besi[de] the banks of the Barmu River. Its inhabitants belonged to a family [of] tribes settled in similar sites along the river valley. The tribes we[re] descended from ancient native peoples who had intermarried with th[e] Indo-Europeans, who arrived later. Fiercely independent, they foug[ht] frequently among themselves and also attacked other settlements, esp[e]cially in times of famine, to seize crops and grazing animals.

Faced with the constant threat of attack, the townspeople took defe[n]sive measures. They encircled their hilltop site with a fortified wa[ll] which combined with the hillside's steep slope to create a bulwa[rk] against surprise attacks. However, the same features that protected t[he] residents made their lives in the town difficult. Sources of water, grazi[ng]

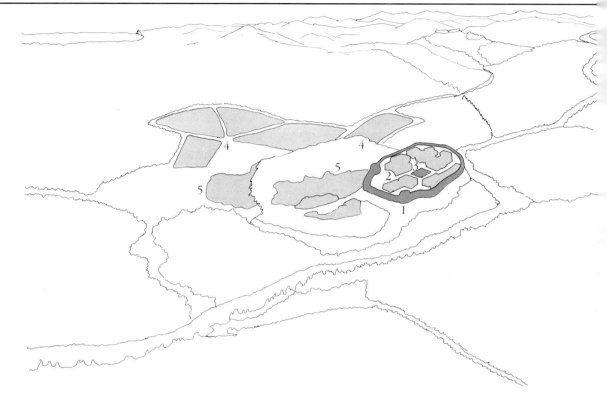

1. Defensive fortifications
An encircling wall protected the town and its inhabitants. The surrounding area was patrolled by one or two sentries. Guards were added during periods of conflict. They watched for hostile forces and, in the event of attack, sounded alarms. Defenders then rushed to man the wall. From its heights they threw stones, shot arrows, and hurled javelins down on the aggressors. The warriors also had armor and swords for protection in close combat.

2. Houses
Dwellings were built on stone foundations and had mud walls. They ranged in width from three to ten feet. Their exact dimensions were determined by the lengths of oak and wild-olive beams that were placed crosswise on top of the walls to support a roof composed of straw, branches, and an upper layer of clay. Each house included a hearth and a venting hole that permitted smoke to escape. A few buildings were two stories tall, and some were used solely to store tools, equipment, and provisions.

3. Silos
An adequate grain supply meant survival. Therefore, safe storage was crucial. The Barmu Valley people dug cylindrical storage areas in the ground and lined them with clay. These silos were then filled with grain and hermetically sealed to preserve the contents. As the people needed grain for food or seed, they opened the silos one by one.

4. Cultivated lands
Near the town lay fields cleared for planting. As successive harvests depleted the soil, the people cleared new stretches of forest. First they burned a wooded area; then they painstakingly extracted the tree roots and repeatedly plowed the ground to ready the new fields.

5. Olive groves and vineyards
Greek people who traded with the settlers introduced the grape and the olive. The townspeople soon added vineyards and olive groves to their cultivated acreage.

The Mediterranean Trinity
Ancient peoples who migrated into southern Europe brought with them knowledge of wheat, grapes, and olives. These crops have been cultivated in the region for centuries, and their products – bread, wine, and oil – form the basis of the Mediterranean diet.

nds, and wood lay beyond the wall and down the hill. The townspeople
d to carry in daily supplies of water and fuel and lead their livestock
ck inside the wall nearly every night.

Most of the townspeople farmed nearby land. Surrounding forests
re cut down to make clearings for cultivation. Because the settlers did
t know the principles of fertilization and crop rotation, their succes-
e harvests eventually exhausted the soil of its nutrients. They then had
abandon the old fields and clear new ones, which were increasingly
stant. Often entire villages resettled on sites closer to virgin land.

The townspeople kept herds of goats and sheep. They also had a few
en, which they used in farm work, and several horses, which their war-
ors rode on reconnaissance tours.

The town's solid stone and clay buildings testified to the construction skills of the Barmu Valley people. All the houses were of similar size and design. They included cisterns for water storage and in-ground silos for grain. The townspeople were acquainted with iron, with which they forged weapons and tools. Because the Barmu Valley was an important route linking disparate regions, trade and commerce between the hilltop settlement and the surrounding communities prospered.

Pre-Roman House
① Stone foundation
② Mud walls
③ Oak and olive beams
④ Hearth
⑤ Loom
⑥ Wooden framework for wall construction
⑦ Roof of beams, branches, and clay
⑧ Basket weaving
⑨ Grindstone
⑩ In-ground silos

Blacksmiths repeatedly ham-
mered the pure iron to increase
its strength. Later they shaped
it on the forge into tools and
weapons. While still red-hot,
these were immersed in water.
They emerged as well-tem-
pered utensils.

on Smelting and Forging
on-rich stones were placed in lay-
s alternating with coal and covered
th clay to create an oven. Air
mped from a bellows caused the
al to burn hotly enough to render
e from the stones.

2. A LEGIONARY CAMP: 2nd Century B.C.

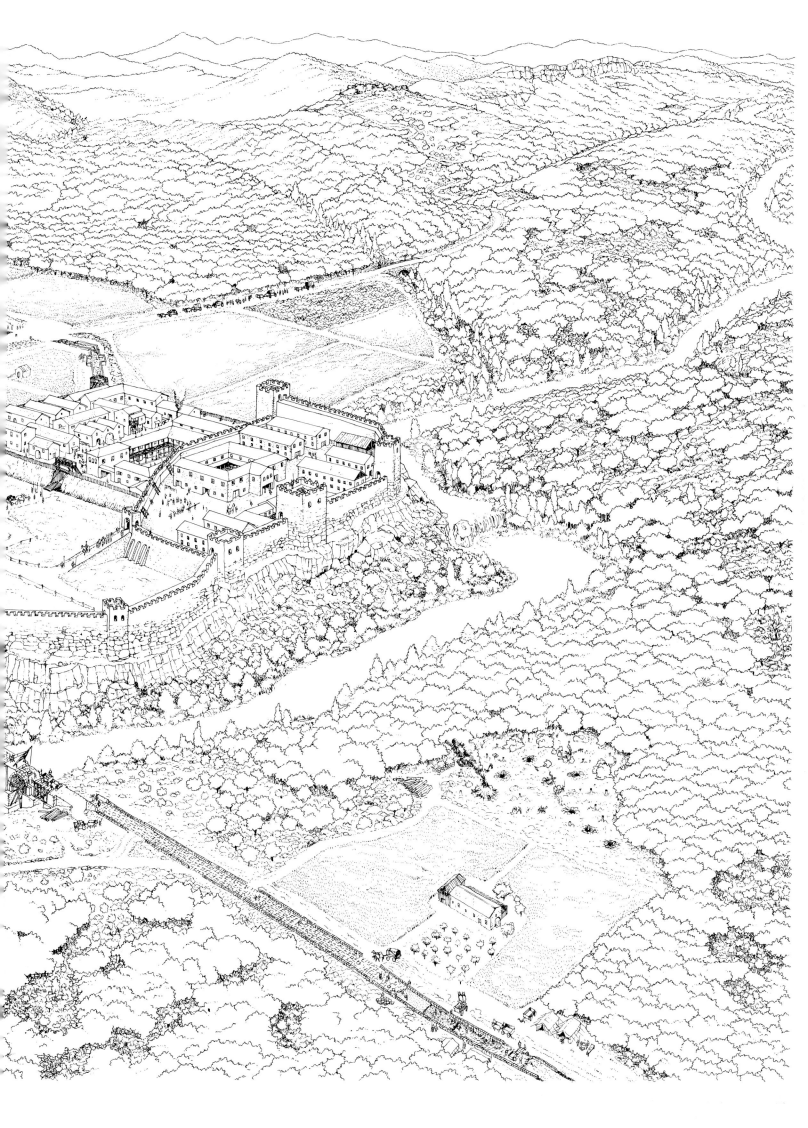

2. A LEGIONARY CAMP
2ND CENTURY B.C.

In 218 B.C. Hannibal's Carthaginian armies crossed the strategic Barm[...] Valley. A conflict of new and terrible proportions rocked the Medite[...] ranean world as the two great powers of the time, the Roman Republ[...] and Carthage, confronted one another in a battle to the death.

After waging a brilliant campaign, Hannibal arrived on the outskirts [...] Rome. Roman troops immediately counterattacked on several front[...] They occupied the Barmu Valley and subjugated the local populac[...] which had allied itself with Carthage. Many valley towns were destroye[...] and their inhabitants scattered. Meanwhile, the Romans built fortresse[...] to halt the advance of reinforcements and supplies that might be sent t[...] Hannibal.

On the hilltop once occupied by farmers and herdsmen, the Roma[...]

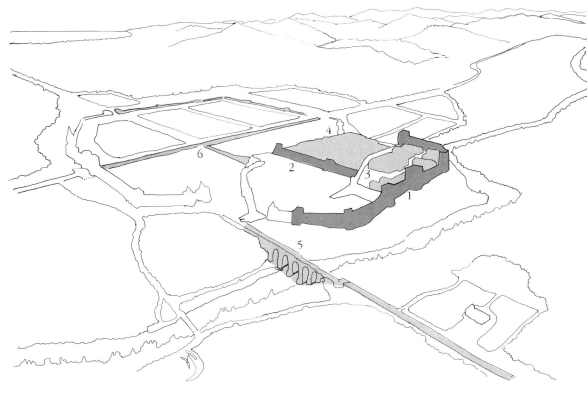

1. Republican ramparts
In the years following the Punic Wars, massive ramparts were erected around some Roman military posts. Huge stone blocks, whose weight held them in place, formed the walls' base. On top of these rested rows of squared boulders bound with a lime, sand, and water mortar.

2. Palisades
The Roman legionaries constructed temporary fortifications around their camps in the form of ditches protected by palisades.

3. Military quarters
When the camps became semipermanent, more comfortable quarters replaced tents. Soldiers were lodged in barracks. Sheds provided shelter for horses, livestock, and armaments. Military commanders were furnished with more spacious quarters.

4. Vicus
Small villages were built in the camp environs to house the families of soldiers, along with merchants and civil servants who moved into the region. During their free hours soldiers visited the vicus for its public baths, taverns, and other amusements.

5. Bridges and roads
To facilitate communications, permit rapid movement of military units, and create new opportunities for trade, the Romans built highways and bridges of bold design. These improvements united the weaker points of their emerging empire. Such conspicuous public works also had considerable propagan- *da value, as they demonstrated Roman ingenuity and power.*

6. City planning
A planning phase preceded the construction of new cities. After studying the resources and needs of the territory, the Romans drew up careful plans. Squads of surveyors laid out road patterns and analyzed how to solve such prob- *lems as supply of provisions and distribution of water.*

Bridge Construction
① Repair of wooden pilings
② Drainage to permit construction of the foundation
③ Construction of supporting piers
④ Construction of arched spans with the aid of wooden framing
⑤ Pulley system (detail)

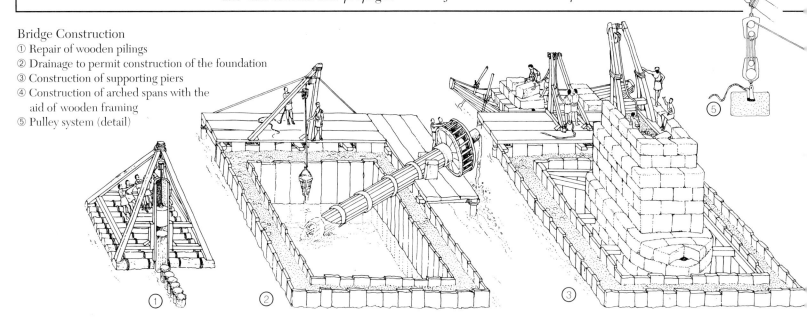

tablished a legionary camp. To protect it they surrounded the encampment with a solid stockade and a ditch. The legionary troops assigned to defend the valley pitched their tents within.

When the second Punic War ended, the Romans kept their military units in place to guarantee control of territories and to preserve them r colonization. Soon the stockade around the Barmu camp was placed with a massive fortified wall; barracks replaced the tents. The ttlement became permanent.

From its base at the Barmu camp, the 9th Legion "Trigemina" force-lly put down all the local people's attempts at rebellion. By the middle the second century B.C., the valley's inhabitants had been completely cified and brought under the control of Rome. Local inhabitants

adopted the language and customs of Roman life. The camp grew to resemble a small city. Soldiers lived within; civil servants, merchants, and soldiers' families resided in the adjoining village, or *vicus*.

Eventually the city was elevated to the status of a colony. The Romans drew up plans for enlargement and improvement to create a center from which they could coordinate all the valley's operations. The legionaries worked around the clock to cut down the surrounding forest. Surveyors and engineers laid out the roadways and limits of the future city. To end dependence on dangerous paths and uncertain fords, military units and slave gangs erected a substantial bridge and built solid Roman roads.

lements of a Stratified Roman Road
Pavimentum, or stone slab surface
Nucleus, or gravel
Rudus, or broken rock
Statumen, or road base
Milestone
Surveyor using a level to calculate angles,
distances, and rectilinears

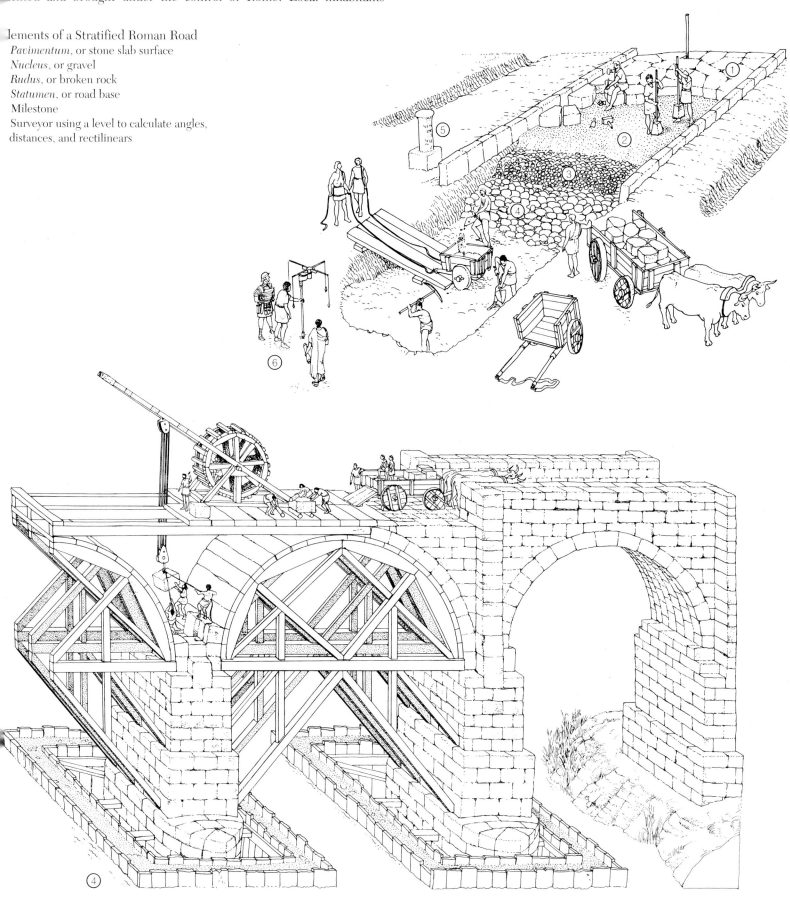

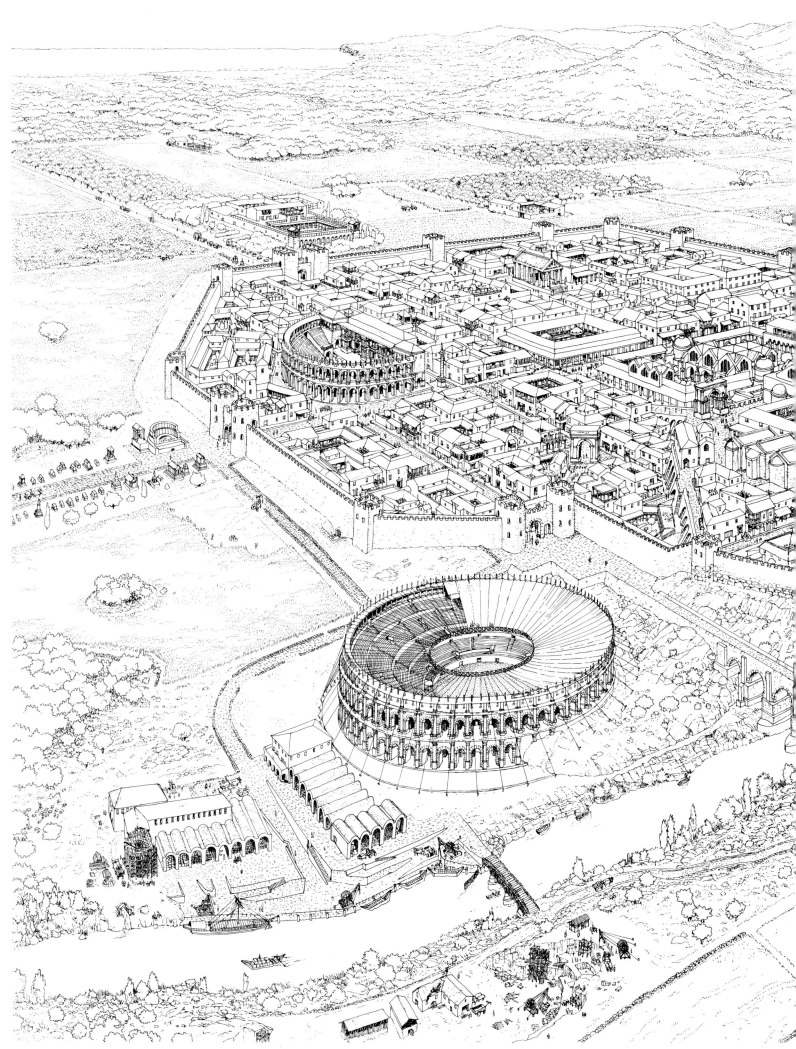

3. A LARGE ROMAN CITY: 2nd Century A.D.

3. A LARGE ROMAN CITY
2ND CENTURY A.D.

In time the Barmu Valley became a Roman province, and the form[er] hilltop camp its most prosperous city-colony. In honor of two of [its] patronesses, the city was called Julia Augusta Barminia Colony, or si[m]ply Barminia.

During the reign of the emperor Trajan in the early second centu[ry] the city achieved its greatest splendor. The area within its walls w[as] totally developed. Its limits had spread to the foot of the hill on whi[ch] the original settlement had been built, and the hillside's precipitous ro[ck] face had been excavated to create three level terraces.

Barminia contained exceptional public buildings and spaces. Th[e] *forum* alone included the temple to Augustus Caesar; the *curia*, or go[v]ernment council chambers; the *basilica*, an assembly building and cou[rt]

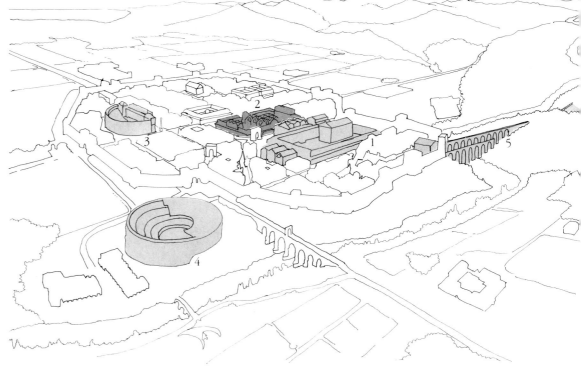

1. Forum
This large square, bounded by arcades, formed the heart of the city. It included the temple; the curia, *in which colonial magistrates and senators met to govern the city; and the* basilica, *the seat of the law courts and some commercial enterprises. The forum offered a natural gathering place where people could stroll and chat. Its arcades provided shade in hot weather and shelter from rain.*

2. Public baths
The Romans valued personal fitness and hygiene. At the public baths, or terme, *they could bathe in heated waters while conversing with friends and associates. Some baths offered gymnastic equipment, massage services, and even libraries. They were ideal places to relax.*

3. Theater
Contemporary dramas and classics of Greek and Roman theater were performed in this building of semicircular design.

4. Amphitheater
Crowds packed this stadium during the presentation of the ludi, *or public games. Gladiator fights* and contests with wild animals were the spectacles most commonly offered. On summer afternoons an enormous canvas, the velarium, *was spread over the amphitheater to shade spectators from the hot sun.*

5. Aqueduct
These elevated conduits provided the city with running water. They drew on springs and rivers situated on higher ground and used the force of gravity to convey water to a storage tower in the city. From there it flowed into a system of smaller ducts and pipes that followed the hill's downward slope. A sewage system flushed discharge and waste water into the river.*

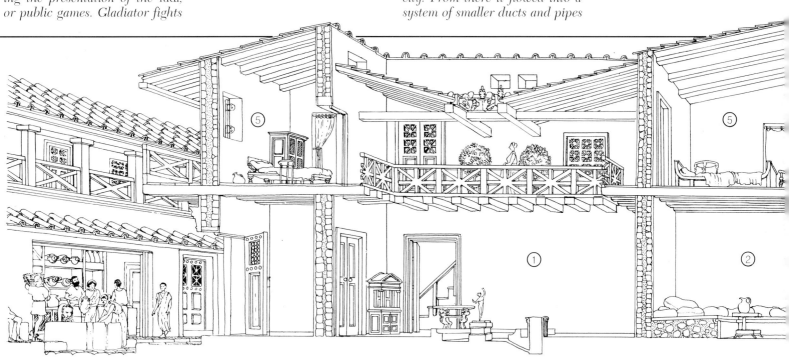

law; and a large portico. In addition, the inner city contained public
[bat]hs and a theater. Outside the walls, Barminia's engineers had used
[th]e hillside's steep slope to advantage and carved from the rock a medi-
[um]-size amphitheater.

[O]f the three landscaped terraces, the uppermost retained its military
[fu]nction. Detachments of the 3rd Legion "Invincible" were quartered
[th]ere, as were the provincial governor's Praetorian guards and various
[ag]encies connected with imperial services. The forum dominated the
[mi]ddle terrace, but space remained for other administrative buildings
[an]d imperial offices, an open-air market, and the homes of the nobility.
[Pu]blic buildings such as the theater and baths stood on the lowest
[ter]race, as did extensive residential districts marked by multistory,

multifamily dwellings called *insulae*, where common people lived. In
this district merchants and artisans operated their stores and workshops.
Barminia's population of 10,000 included Roman citizens, freemen,
slaves, and foreigners.

Beyond the city walls, a port had been built on the Barmu. Wine, olive
oil, ceramics, and other local wares passed through it on their way to the
Mediterranean. A broad Roman road crossed a bridge of imposing proportions to arrive at Barminia's eastern gate. The city's other major
gateways opened onto the northern, western, and southern highways.

A number of small farming towns had sprung up in the city's environs.
The region's cultivated lands had been divided into large quadrangular
lots, from which Barminia reaped plentiful harvests.

[In]sula, or Multistory, Multifamily Dwelling

[①]Fountain   ⑥ *Termopilium*, or tavern
[②]Sewage pipes   ⑦ Apartments
[③]Fresh water duct
[④]Artisan's workshop
[⑤]Butcher shop

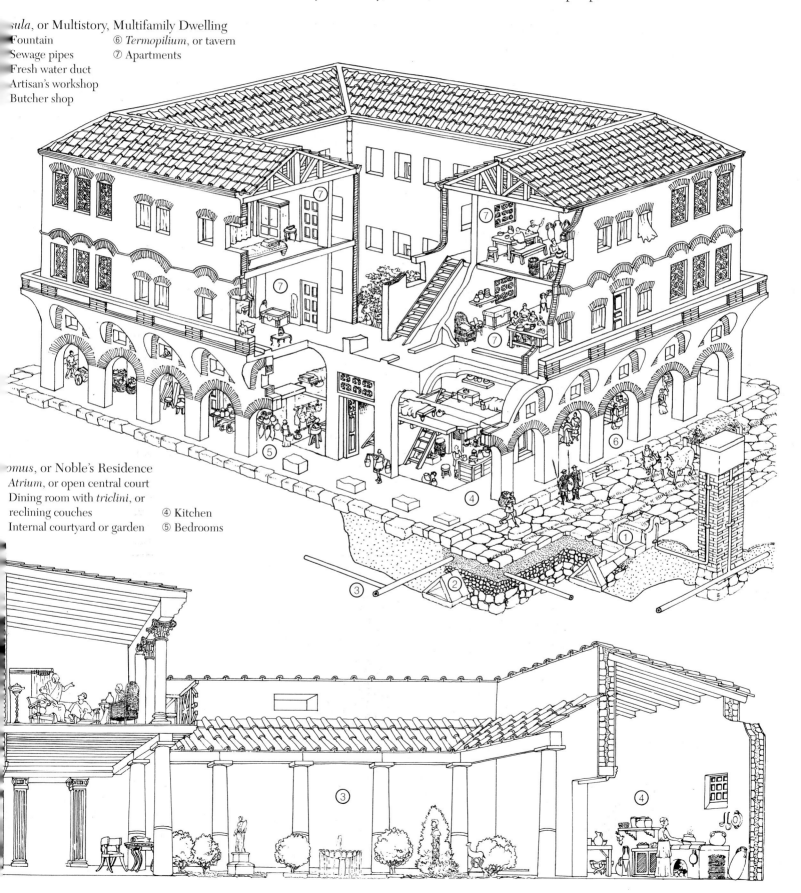

[D]omus, or Noble's Residence

[①]*Atrium*, or open central court
[②]Dining room with *triclini*, or
     reclining couches   ④ Kitchen
[③]Internal courtyard or garden   ⑤ Bedrooms

4. THE AGE OF THE BARBARIANS: 6th Century

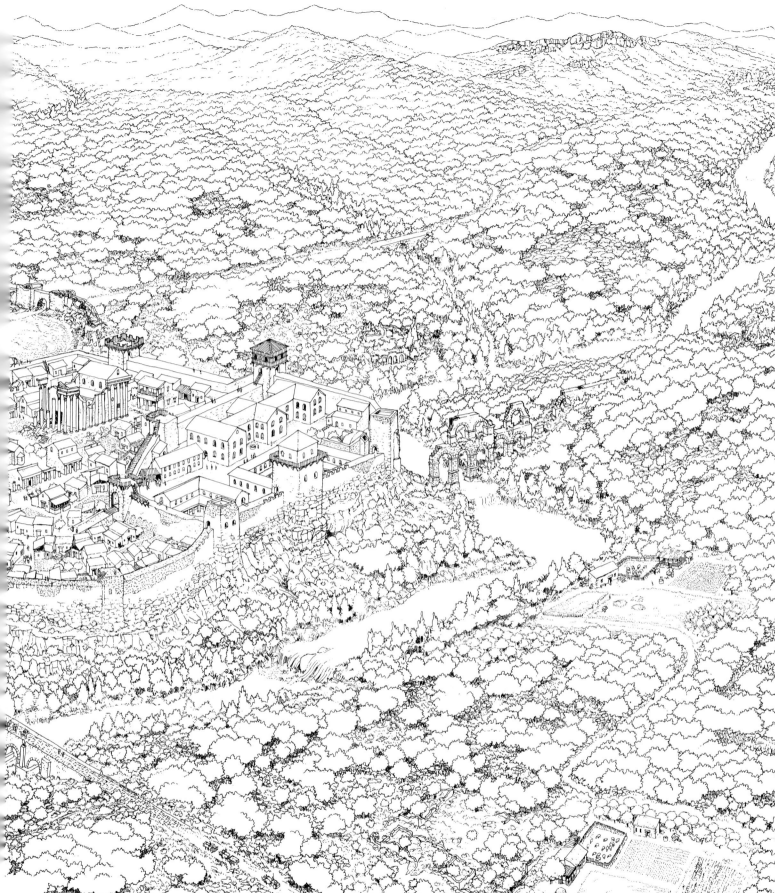

4. THE AGE OF THE BARBARIANS
6TH CENTURY

Although life in Barminia remained peaceful for decades, the Roman Empire's gradual decay finally affected it. At the end of the third cent[ury] the city suffered a violent invasion by barbarian tribes, which the emp[ire] had been unable to stop from infiltrating its northern borders. Barmi[nia] was completely destroyed. Survivors struggled to refortify the city us[ing] materials salvaged from the ruins.

Barbarians were not the only threat. The empire was being shaken [to] its foundations by internal economic and social crises. Urban uprisi[ngs] and peasant revolts signaled decades of civil war and social strife [to] come. The emergence and spread of a new religion, Christianity, prov[id]ed a moderating influence but could not halt the empire's slow decay.

In the fourth century, as the empire was rocked by successive cris[es]

1. Palace stronghold
The barbarian leader built his fortress-residence on the remains of earlier buildings. The glorious architectural tradition of Rome vanished. The new buildings were crudely designed, with rough stone walls, narrow doorways, and a few small windows.

2. Basilica and baptistry
By the time Constantine became Roman emperor the Christian religion had spread so widely that during his reign (A.D. 306 – 337) he converted and made Christianity the official religion. Members of the church hierarchy wielded considerable influence and in the empire's last phases frequently became powerful political figures. The basilica was the spacious structure where the pious met to celebrate Christian rites. Its design was based on that of the old Roman assembly hall and law court, which was deemed more suitable to the practice of the new religion than the ancient pagan temples. Baptism, the rite of immersion in water, was practiced in the baptistry, at the rear of the basilica.

3. New ramparts
As the city's population dwindled, so did its physical limits. The populace retreated to the upper ground, which was the most easily defensible. A new fortified wall was built on the remains of the old one, using materials salvaged from its ruins. The damaged Roman ramparts that remained standing were carefully restored and reinforced.

4. New churches
During the sixth century an additional basilica was erected on the site of the old amphitheater. It was dedicated to the martyrs St. Argenio and St. Eulalie, who were said to have been sacrificed in the Roman circuses of the third century.

5. Roman ruins
The majority of public and private Roman buildings had been destroyed in battle, by fire, or simply through abandonment. As time passed, Barminians began to treat the ruins as quarries from which to extract construction materials. Some vital structures, such as the ramparts and bridges, were carefully maintained or restored. The loss of the aqueducts deprived the city of its water supply. As a result, wells were dug and cisterns were buil[t] to provide new water source[s] and storage facilities.

Early Christian Basilica
Basilicas and their baptistries were the structures that typified Christianity during the late empire and the ascendancy of the barbarian kingdoms. The entire Christian community gathered there to celebrate religious rites.

① Baptistry
② Baptismal font
③ Nave
④ Apse
⑤ Wooden trusswork to support roof

colonies lost their standing as centers of commerce. The quality of
[Rom]an life deteriorated dramatically. Cities became unsafe as the Roman
[arm]y lost its ability to guarantee the defense of frontiers.

[B]arminia vividly mirrored the empire's decline. The population had
[dw]indled to a mere 3,000 inhabitants at the close of the fourth century.
[Ho]uses and public buildings stood in ruins. Their crumbling remains
[pr]ovided materials for makeshift shelters.

[B]y the mid-fifth century, the old Roman Empire had splintered into a
[nu]mber of barbarian kingdoms. One of these absorbed Barminia, and in
[the] sixth century a barbarian ruler established his palace stronghold in
[the] city. From that site he and his warriors controlled the entire Barmu
[Val]ley region. They refortified the city's upper terrace and based their

armies there. The civilian population resided on the middle terrace,
close to the Christian basilica, which had been erected during the reign
of the emperor Constantine. The city's lower terrace, long since aban-
doned, remained in ruins.

Most of the city's 1,500 inhabitants and the majority of people in the
surrounding region were of Roman descent. They continued to follow
Roman customs, maintaining the language and the culture. The barbarian warriors and their families constituted a controlling minority. Their
first priority was waging war against the Byzantine Empire, which
sought during this period to extend its influence into the strategically
situated Barmu Valley.

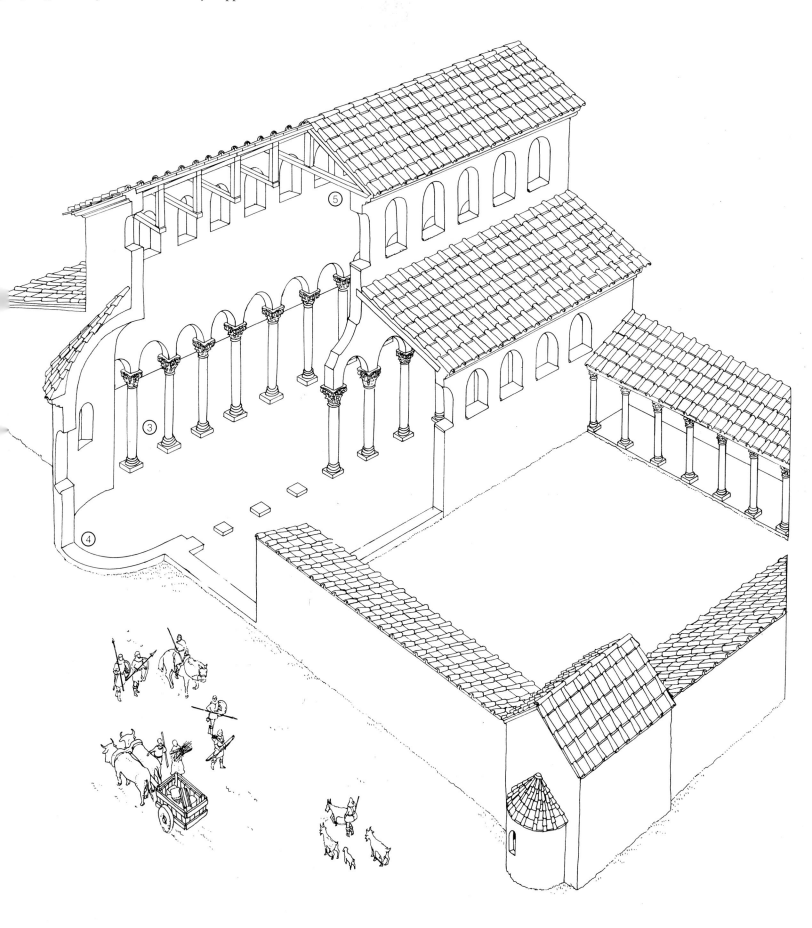

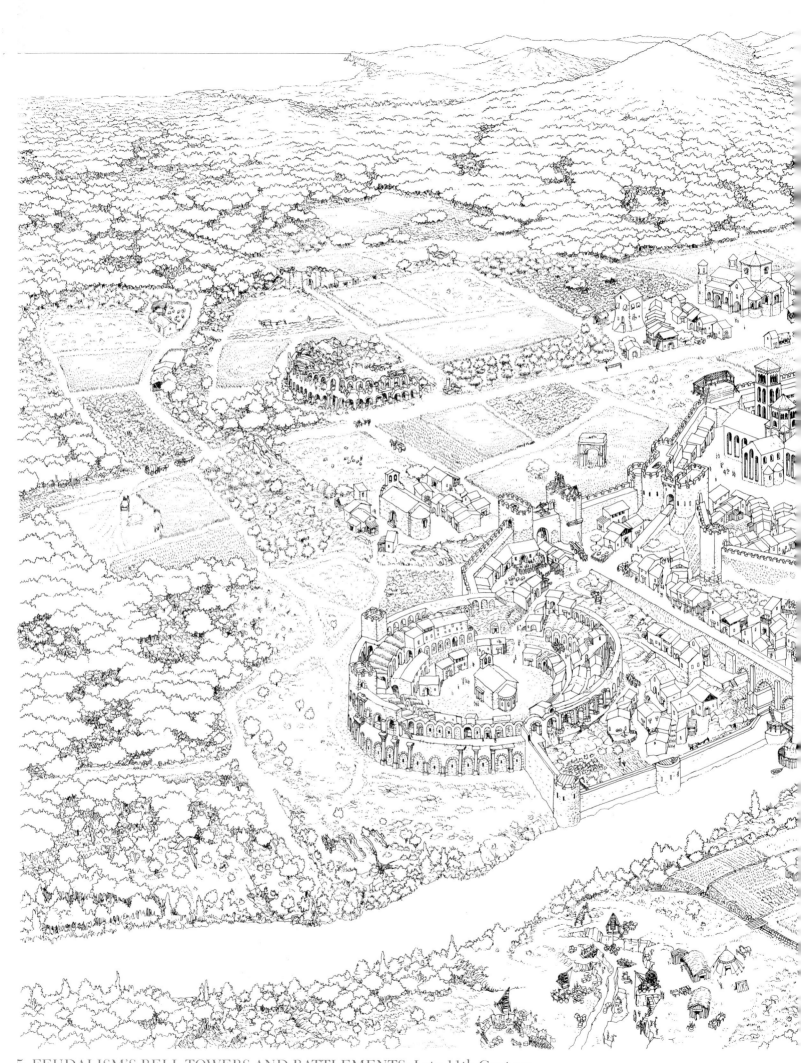

5. FEUDALISM'S BELL TOWERS AND BATTLEMENTS: Late 11th Century

5. FEUDALISM'S BELL TOWERS AND BATTLEMENTS
LATE 11TH CENTURY

Barminia languished for centuries. Successive wars laid waste to the c[...] However, the geographic site and massive fortifications that made it [...] important strategic center ensured that a small number of inhabita[...] continued to live there.

In the early ninth century Barminia belonged to Charlemagn[...] empire. The Franks maintained a garrison in the city to assure their co[...] trol of the region. When the Frankish empire in its turn crumbled, [...] was replaced throughout Europe by a proliferation of feudal fiefdoms.

By the close of the eleventh century Barminia, now called Barmi, w[...] the center of an emerging feudal dukedom. Classical Latin evolved in[...] a new language. Roman culture and customs were also transformed, in[...] an entirely new social order. A small group of nobles and ecclesiasti[...]

1. Ducal palace
This fortified residence, built on the ruins of older buildings, was eventually renovated to conform with Romanesque aesthetics and construction techniques. It contained an arcaded courtyard from which one passed into the duke's living quarters, the stables, the palace guard's quarters, and the chapel.

2. Cathedral
This was the most important church of the diocese and one of the most significant components of the medieval city. Typically, it had vast dimensions and majestic form. Nearby stood the administrative buildings and residences of the bishop and other church officials.

3. Monasteries
Monastic life was critical in shaping society during the Middle Ages. Monasteries stood outside the city walls on sites traditionally associated with the deaths of martyred saints. They were self-sufficient centers possessed of lands, granaries, and mills. Their libraries were the period's true repositories of culture. In them *monks patiently copied ancient texts of science, philosophy, and religion.*

4. Hydraulic mill
The use of hydraulic power became widespread during the *High Middle Ages. Typically, this energy powered flour mills. The flow of rushing water activated large wheels whose motion transferred the energy through axles and cogwheels to millstones.* These stones ground grain into *flour. Mills were generally the property of feudal lords, who exacted a tax for their use.*

Hydraulic Flour Mill
① Waterwheel
② Millstone
③ Millstream

Fortified Romanesque House
Stone barbicans ① like awnings protected doorways and windows and made defense easier. Chimneys were not yet in common use; instead, smoke was vented through a flue cut into the wall behind the hearth ②.

minated this rural society and acted with nearly total political inde-
ndence.

The duke of Barmi chose the city's highest ground as the site of his
tified palace. There he installed the territory's administrative offices.
e city limits expanded to provide living space for Barmi's 3,000 inhab-
nts. At the start of the eleventh century, the early Christian basilica
s torn down and construction began on a splendid Romanesque
hedral. The bishop erected a residential palace from which to govern
e Barmi diocese. Although a few market gardens and vacant tracts
mained, most of the land within the city walls was urbanized. Artisans
the service of the church or the duke lived within the city, as did some
the peasants who worked the lands outside the walls. A small Jewish

community operated commercial and financial concerns.

Beyond the city walls, new churches served as the centers of develop-
ing suburbs. Two monasteries housed active religious communities
whose members prayed, worked the land, and produced accomplished
works of art, theology, and philosophy.

To promote agriculture, the duke ordered the construction of irriga-
tion canals. Water-powered flour mills sprang up along the length of the
river. Trade throughout the region increased. Barmi, at the region's center, grew rapidly.

omanesque Church
Nave
Apse
Tambour and cupola atop
pendentives
Stone-and-mortar vault
Semicircular arch
Pillar
Buttress
Scaffolding and framework for
construction of a vault
Stonecutters and carpenters, the
principal craftsmen of the project,
at work under the direction of the
master builder

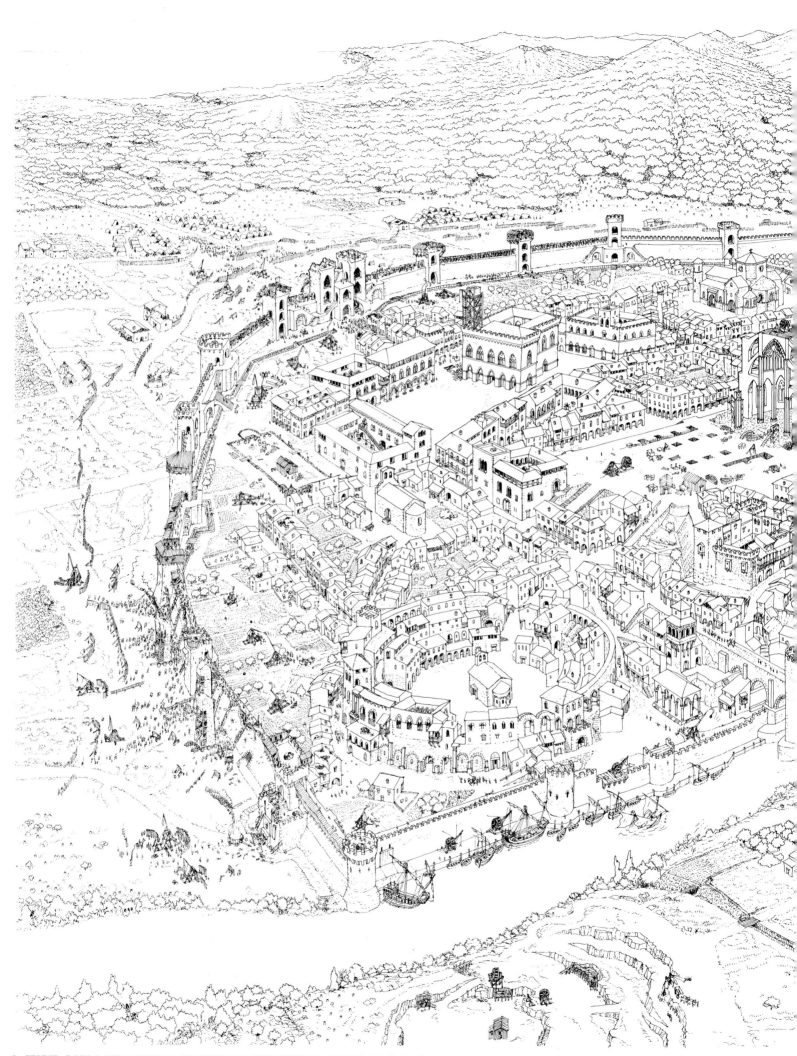

6. THE CULMINATION OF THE MEDIEVAL CITY: Mid-13th Century

6. THE CULMINATION OF THE MEDIEVAL CITY
MID-13TH CENTURY

Barmi grew rapidly during the twelfth and thirteenth centuries. Artisan workshops proliferated. The district's wines and oils, the woolen cloth manufactured in city workshops, and the arms forged in local ironwork all assured a prosperous trade. Barmi's production was exported to distant regions. Meanwhile, the commercial traffic that had developed from one end of the Mediterranean to the other brought exotic new wares and essentials to the city.

By the mid-thirteenth century, Barmi had 7,000 inhabitants. A river port was built to increase trade, and a new canal system made navigation easier. Since the city interior was almost entirely developed, townspeople began to construct new roads beyond the walls to encourage development of outlying areas. Populous towns and villages sprang up

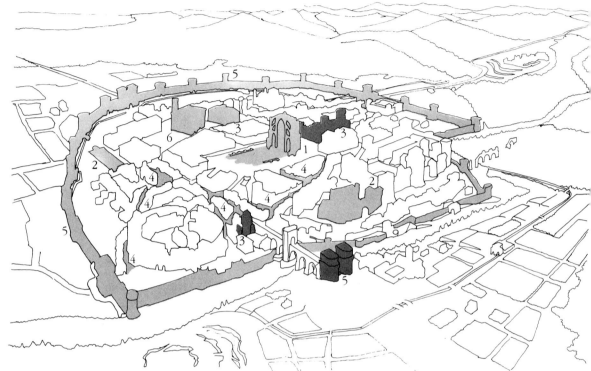

1. Cathedral
During the thirteenth and fourteenth centuries a new style of architecture spread throughout Western Europe: the Gothic. Many new cathedrals were built according to the new aesthetic, while a number of Romanesque cathedrals and churches were enlarged, remodeled, or completed following Gothic principles.

2. Monasteries and convents
In the thirteenth century a new type of religious building appeared both inside and on the outskirts of Mediterranean cities. The monasteries and convents of mendicant religious orders often grew to occupy substantial tracts. Council decrees were sometimes passed to limit construction of their churches, cloisters, outbuildings, orchards, and market gardens within the city.

3. Nobles' palaces
Some noblemen and a few rich merchants who had achieved the rank of nobles built urban palaces as family residences. These mansions included courtyards and numerous outbuildings. Their soaring towers rivaled the bell towers and came to symbolize the city.

4. Artisans' lanes
Craftspeople who followed the same trade operated their workshops in particular streets or districts, and the streets came to be known by the names of the trades. Artisans united in professional organizations called guilds. They held meetings in guildhalls built for that purpose; charters and bylaws were also maintained there.

5. Ramparts
As the city grew, its fortified walls were enlarged. In this way the urban center guaranteed its defenses and its citizens' independence. Strictly patrolled gates gave sentries the opportunity to monitor all individuals who entered and exited the city.

6. City hall
The townspeople's self-governing body, the council, lost no time in erecting an impressive building to house its assemblies and to provide space for offices and public archives. As time passed and the wealth of cities increased, city halls grew ever more opulent.

Defense and Siege of a City
① The city gates were protected by towers and complicated drawbridges.
② Battlements and corbeled arches allowed defenders to rain arrows and rocks on aggressors.
③ Catapults and ballistae were used by both attackers and defenders of the walls.
④ Attackers tunneled toward the ramparts. Once a breach was made in the wall, the underpinnings were set on fire.

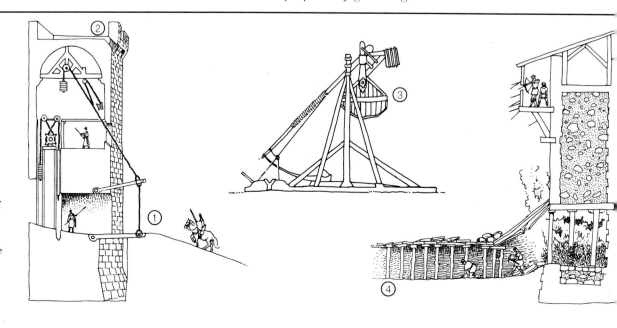

ound Barmi and eventually surrounded it on all sides.

The duke actively promoted trade, and in exchange for oaths of allegiance he ceded to his subjects certain rights of self-government. Townspeople organized a city council, which ruled on local issues and problems. This transfer of power marked the emergence of city-states. The council ordered the construction of new ramparts. It also commissioned construction of a new square to house an impressive city hall, which stood as a symbol of the townspeople's increased power.

By the early thirteenth century the city had grown too populous for the Romanesque cathedral to accommodate all worshipers. In response to the bishop's call for a new church, tradespeople, artisans' guilds, and nobles alike offered to collaborate on the enterprise, with contributions of all types. The new cathedral was designed in the Gothic style. Its construction continued for 112 years.

Meanwhile, new kinds of religious buildings appeared within the city walls: the monasteries and convents of mendicant orders. A small hospital for the poor was built; in time it would become the city's general hospital. Some buildings near the city hall were adapted to house the lecture halls and lodgings of a university destined to gain renown for its school of medicine. Only a few minor sieges and external religious conflicts disturbed Barmi's peace. At the close of the century, however, the church mounted a campaign of persecution of Jews and others deemed heretics. These people were expelled and their homes were destroyed.

Construction of a
Gothic Cathedral
① *Ogive*, or Gothic arch with
   pointed vault
② Stained glass window
③ Buttress
④ Gutter
⑤ Flying buttress
⑥ *Pinnacle*, or pyramidal spire
   atop a buttress
⑦ Block and tackle
⑧ Naves
⑨ Carpenters
⑩ Stonecutters, sculptors, and
   glassblowers

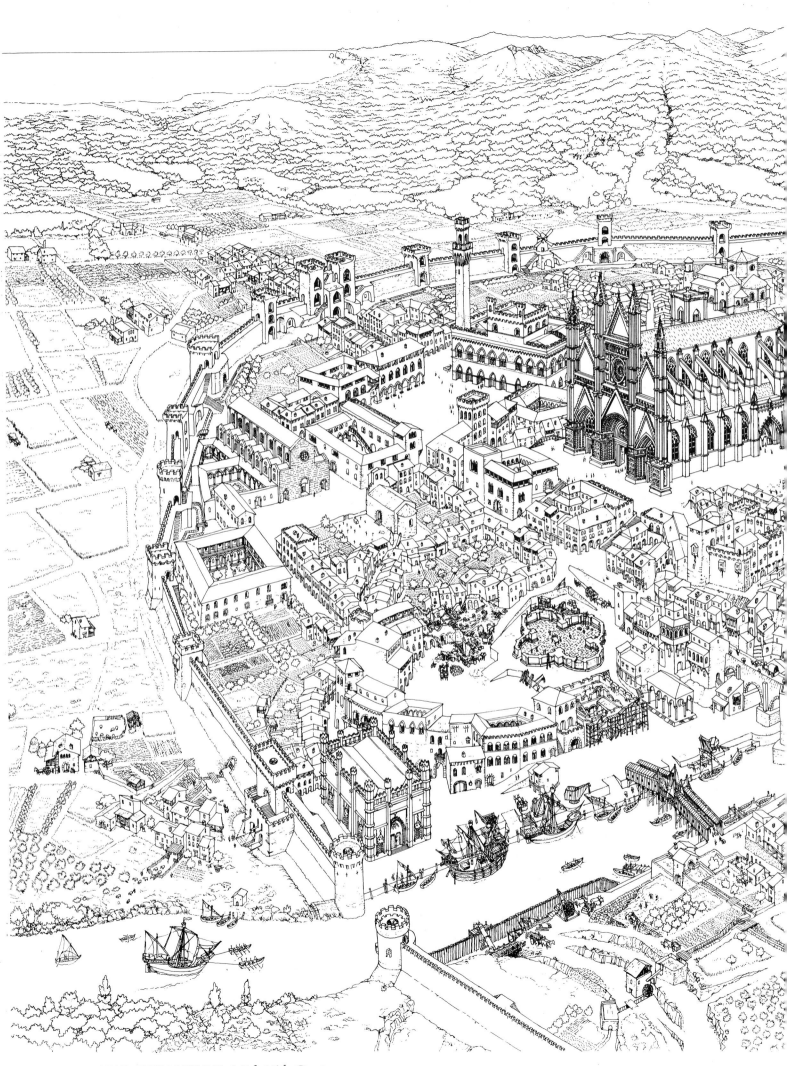

7. COMMERCIAL EXPANSION: Mid-15th Century

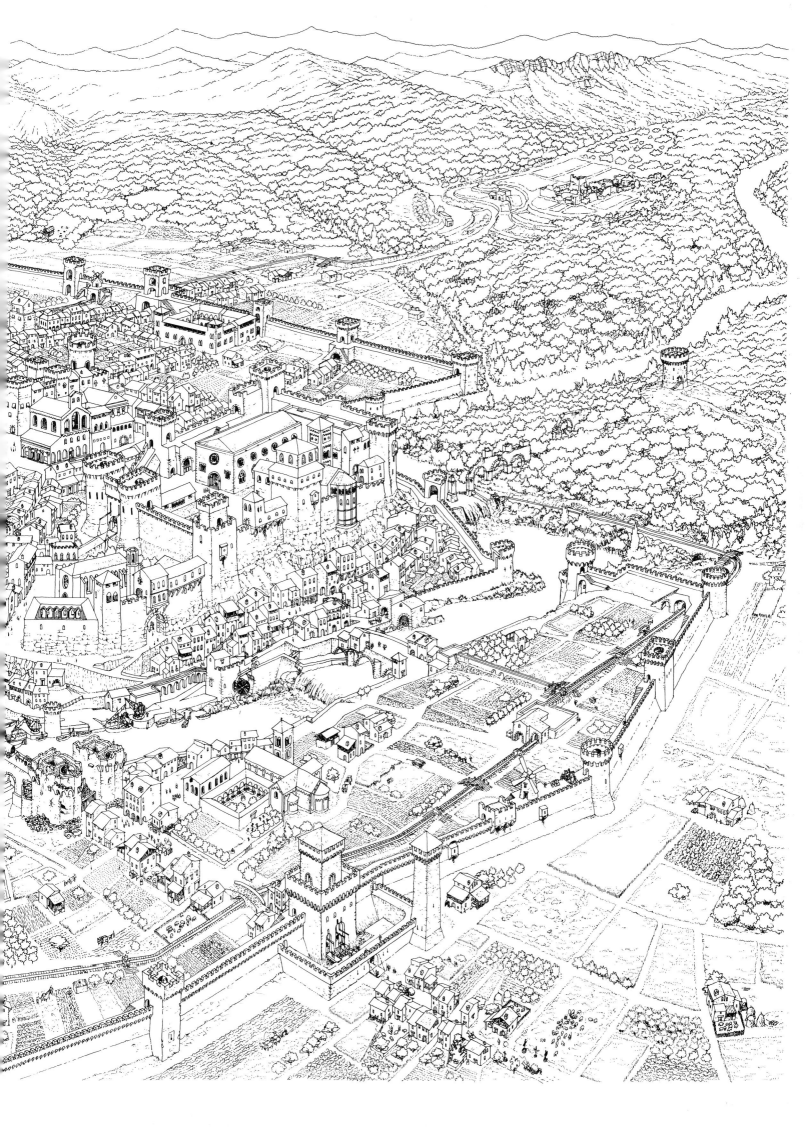

7. COMMERCIAL EXPANSION
MID-15TH CENTURY

During the fifteenth century Barmi continued to grow, but at a m[ore] modest rate. The devastating plagues and epidemics that afflic[ted] Western Europe slowed the growth of Barmi's population, as did seve[ral] bloody uprisings, civil wars, and other struggles for control of the city. [By] the mid-fifteenth century Barmi had a population of 14,000. Its physi[cal] expansion continued: within the city walls, large cultivated tracts we[re] converted to building lots, and the walls themselves were extended [to] take in the district that had grown up on the opposite bank of the riv[er.] They were further enlarged to make room for anticipated growth in [the] future.

The city undertook a major redevelopment program. The city hall w[as] enlarged and given a new façade. To complement it, a new square w[as]

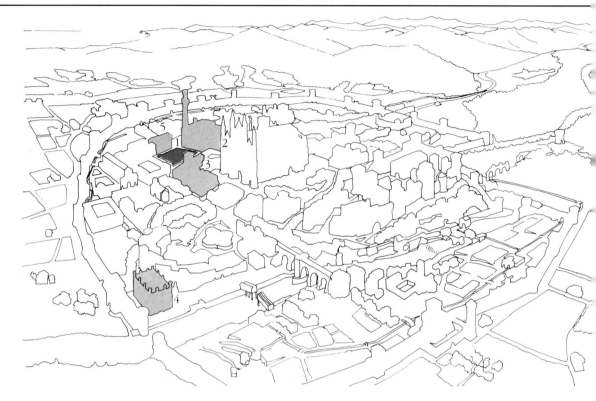

1. Main square
As the forum had been the vital city center in Roman times, so the main square was now. The city hall was its dominant presence. Its porticoes allowed pedestrians to stroll in comfort in any weather. The broad open spaces of the square furnished sites for markets, tournaments, and festivals.

2. City hall
Beginning in the thirteenth century, the city hall became one of Barmi's most visible and important buildings. As the city prospered, its citizens lavished funds for improvements on the building. It contained the offices of public representatives and a large assembly hall for council meetings and social gatherings. The regular tolling of a mechanized clock on the building's impressive tower announced the hours and gave pattern to the working day.

3. University
The curriculum of the medieval university included theology, law, canonical law, philosophy, grammar, rhetoric, Greek, Latin, and medicine. There were lecture halls and rooms adapted to spe-cialized studies, as well as lodgings for both faculty and students.

4. Mercantile exchange
The merchants' hall was a cavernous building where dealers displayed goods and bargained over prices. Only the largest commercial centers had exchanges of this size.

5. Financial exchange
The development of urban commerce in the early Middle Ages brought the first financial enti-ties. These forerunners of moder[n] banks extended loans, acted a[s] guarantors, held funds o[n] deposit, and offered a number o[f] other financial services.

Tower Houses
Quarrels and rivalries prompted many wealthy and noble families to build houses in the form of towers. Such stone fortresses were easy to defend in the case of attack. Branches of a single family often combined to create concentrations of allied tower houses.

out. This soon became the city's nerve center, its arcades and porti-
s serving as the site of outdoor markets and annual festivals.
wever, it was not the only place in the city suited to popular gather-
s: church squares were used both as cemeteries and as informal
eting places. Convents and monasteries were remodeled during this
iod and in some cases greatly enlarged.

rade continued lively, despite the turbulent times. Its proceeds paid
the construction of new palaces and the renovation of existing ones.
ere space was scarce, multistory houses of ever increasing height
re built. Signs of prosperity were apparent everywhere. The labor
ce had work in abundance.

ity services improved, as did the urban infrastructure. New sewers
were built, and new springs increased the supply of water to Barmi's
fountains. Garbage collection was also instituted.

Meanwhile, the river was channeled into large hydraulic plants.
Industries that could benefit from water power, such as paper-making
and textile concerns, opened workshops on the banks of the river.

The city's main gate was enlarged and improved. The imposing Gothic
building that rose just inside it, the mercantile exchange, served as a
symbol of the merchants' wealth and power. The merchants' district,
facing the port, increased in grandeur and opulence until it became one
of the most dynamic and prestigious areas in Barmi.

For all practical purposes, the city's expansion was now finished.
Within the walls, undeveloped land was virtually nonexistent.

Artisan's House and Workshop

① Sample of goods produced and sold
② Well
③ Kitchen garden
④ Hearth
⑤ Kitchen
⑥ Workshop
⑦ Attic
⑧ Pantry
⑨ Bedrooms

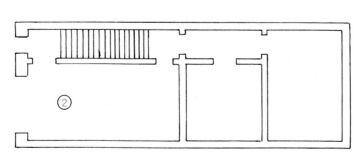

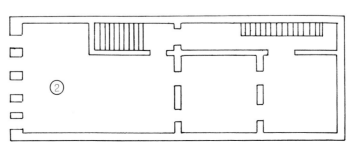

Artisan's House

The craftsperson's house included a workshop, sales space, and living quarters. A sample of the artisan's product was displayed outside the front door. The master artisan and his assistants worked on the ground floor, and the assistants, the artisan, and his family lived on the upper floors.

Artisans' dwellings were usually row houses that shared common supporting walls. Behind each house was a small yard containing a kitchen garden and a well, generous enough to provide all the water needed for work and family consumption. Beginning in the thirteenth century, nearly all urban houses contained hearths for cooking and heat.

① Façade
② Interior floor plan

8. THE FLOWERING OF THE RENAISSANCE: Early 16th Century

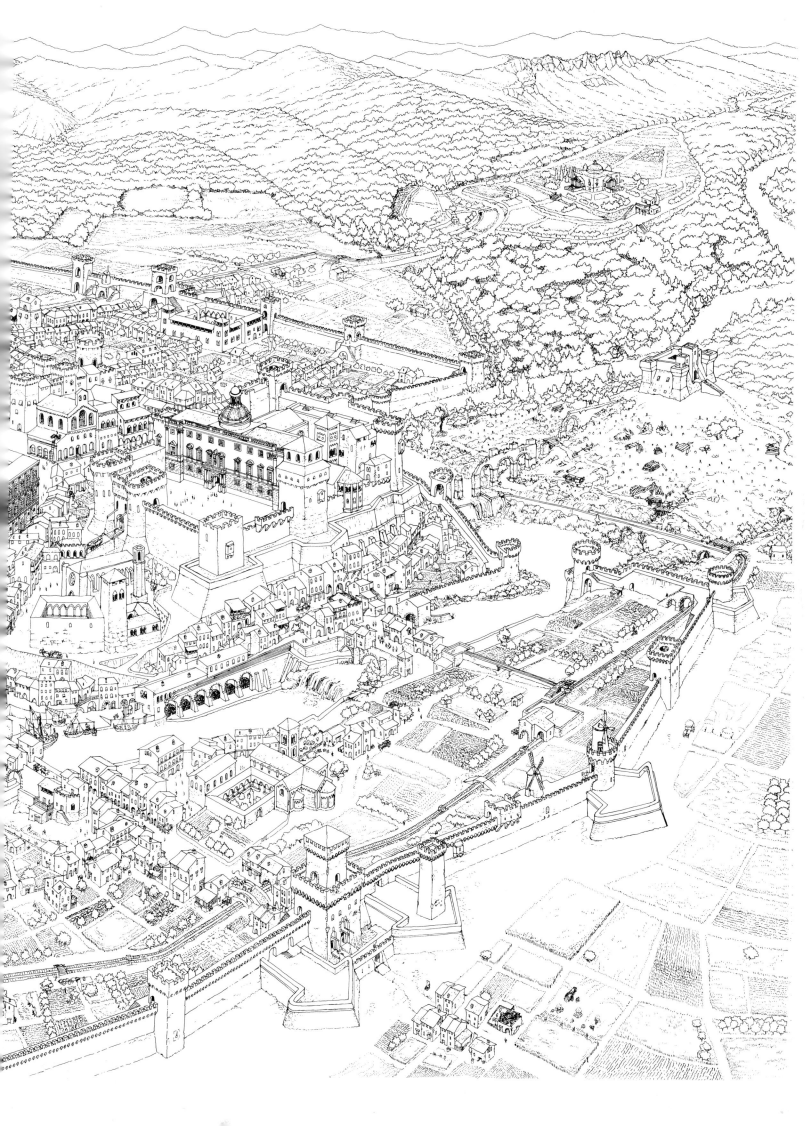

8. THE FLOWERING OF THE RENAISSANCE
EARLY 16TH CENTURY

Near the close of the fifteenth century, Barmi ended its physical expansion and entered a stable phase. In contrast, the political climate was convulsive. Several families vied for supremacy within the city, while a number of European princes strove to gain control of the lower Barmi Valley and annex it to their territories. These chronic struggles, combined with the epidemics of the late Middle Ages, stalled population growth. By the early sixteenth century the city had 17,000 inhabitants, thanks to a continued influx of peoples from the surrounding region.

In spite of the political situation, the city maintained its prosperity. Technologies were perfected, new workshops opened, and merchants profited from both the wars and the internal struggles.

Because the city had arrived at the limits defined by its medieval

1. Palaces
During the Renaissance, the wealth and influence of merchants as a group increased. They joined with powerful aristocrats to form a social class that dominated the city's political life. As symbols of their power, members of this class commissioned imposing palaces and townhouses in the most advanced architectural styles.

2. Religious buildings
Renaissance architects built spectacular churches that typically incorporated a domed cupola and design features copied from Greek and Roman temples. Some existing churches were enlarged or remodeled according to Renaissance design standards.

3. Public works
One of the liveliest concerns of public officials was the reorganization and design of urban space. Public services were expanded, and streets and squares were adapted to meet the new needs of the city.

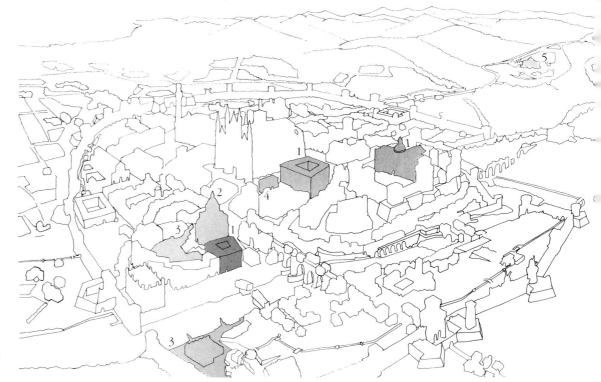

4. Mint
In this facility Barmi struck its own currency. Coins were cast in gold, silver, and bronze. The mint included a foundry and all machinery necessary to the task.

5. Farm towns
A few powerful landowners undertook programs to modernize their rural holdings. They built splendid mansions that, although functional, looked more

like palaces than farmhouses.

Renaissance Church
① Lantern
② Domed cupola
③ Tambour
④ Pendentive

lls, urban renovation during the second half of the fifteenth century used on embellishing, refining, and perfecting it. Teams of engineers, chitects, sculptors, painters, and craftspeople of every sort combined alter the face of Barmi drastically in a very brief time.

The city council competed with prominent families and the church to onsor major decorative and architectural works. The most ambitious oject undertaken was the construction of a vast new church dedicated St. Eulalie. Barmi's streets were improved and its squares, especially ose near the gate, were beautified. New fountains were scattered roughout the city, and the mansions of socially emergent families and eady prominent ones lined the avenues. The elegance of the new uctures offered a sharp contrast to the out-of-fashion Gothic ones.

The frequent wars made additional fortifications necessary, as battles occasionally approached the city walls. Aggressors had changed their siege tactics, and the urban artillery needed new defensive concepts to match. Barmi's ramparts were reinforced with platforms and strongholds where defensive artillery could be positioned. An additional fortress was set on a nearby hilltop to defend the districts that lay beyond the river. The former ducal palace, now the residence of an influential family under the protection of a European prince, was remodeled to serve a strategic defensive function.

By the opening of the sixteenth century, Barmi had undergone a qualitative change; it had evolved into a modern city.

Palace of a Wealthy Merchant Family
① Courtyard
② Well
③ Kitchen
④ Study/library
⑤ Loggia
⑥ Bedroom suite

9. A FORTIFIED CITY: Mid-17th Century

9. A FORTIFIED CITY
MID-17TH CENTURY

During the sixteenth and seventeenth centuries absolute monarchs co[n]solidated power throughout Europe. Their interminable territor[ial] disputes regularly led to armed conflict. Barmi found itself, in the m[id]dle of the sixteenth century, in the orbit of a particular Europe[an] kingdom. The Barmu Valley's wealth and strategic importance, howe[ver] made it a region contested by many powers claiming sovereignty.

The nearby frontier represented a constant source of anxiety [to] Barmians. To defend it, the city was often forced to garrison troops d[is]patched by the king. Where necessary, the medieval ramparts we[re] reinforced. Bastions rose, and a broad moat with a covered walkway a[nd] a *glacis*, or slope of debris, was excavated as the first line of defense. T[he] new fortifications were designed to distance attackers and protect t[he]

1. Fortified citadels
To protect the city's weak points and its principal defenses, subsidiary fortifications were built. These fortresses and citadels armed with artillery were difficult to storm.

2. Baroque gate
As in preceding centuries, a few gates permitted entrance to the city. Those that existed were defended by a system of coordinated fortifications. This gate exemplifies the baroque style much used in military architecture of the seventeenth century.

3. Bastions
These projecting ramparts were fundamental components of the modernized city walls. In them the bulk of the artillery was deployed to fire on anyone who represented a threat to the walls. Bastions were carefully positioned to ensure total coverage of the surrounding area.

4. Moat
The moat forced attacking armies to cross an exposed area where defenders could freely fire on

them. It lay between the ramparts and the sustaining wall that, with the glacis, formed the first line of defense. In some cases it was filled with water; in others it was left dry.

5. Governor's palace
The former ducal palace became the governor's residence and the principal building of the city's militarized center. This fortified complex formed a small citadel.

6. Baroque church
A limited number of religiou[s] buildings and palaces were buil[t] or remodeled according to the baroque style in vogue during the seventeenth century.

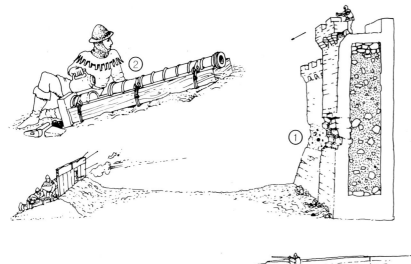

Artillery and Fortifications
During the sixteenth century artillery was notably improved. Consequently, the old *medieval ramparts* ① became easy targets for direct *cannon fire* ②. In the seventeenth and eighteenth centuries many medieval ramparts were reinforced or rebuilt according to new designs. Broad *moats* ③ or ditches, which could be defended from *parapets* ④, were dug. The ramparts were furnished with *bastions* ⑤ from which defensive artillery was fired down on aggressors. A broad *glacis* ⑥, or slope of debris (talus), protected the walls from enemy artillery fire. These new defensive measures made the siege of a fortified city a slow and very difficult undertaking.

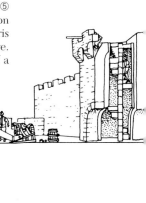

y from direct artillery fire. In contrast to the old medieval ramparts, new complex stood nearly a thousand feet wide.

Jnfortunately, the fortifications were put to the test. Once in the late teenth century and twice in the first half of the seventeenth, hostile nies laid siege the city for long, difficult months. In the course of the al siege, hostile infantry succeeded in breaching the ramparts and unting an assault. The city was sacked. Some buildings burned to the und, and hundreds of inhabitants perished at the hands of enemy sol- rs.

n spite of their precarious situation, the Barmians remained an indus- us people and their city a center of lively trade. The city continued to w, and by the mid-seventeenth century many artisans had substan-

tially enlarged their workshops. The river port continued as active as it had been. Production diversified. Textiles remained important, but now cotton as well as woolen cloth was manufactured. Meanwhile, ironworks limited their production to wartime necessities. Paper, glassware, and assorted other products occupied important positions in the local econo-my.

Excluding improvements made to the city's defenses, few public pro-jects were undertaken inside the fortified city. Construction was limited to a few buildings, palaces, and churches. These were designed accord-ing to the architectural styles fashionable at the time of their construction – first mannerism, then the baroque.

Siege Tactics

As new defensive strategies developed, so did tactics to overcome them. Enemy engineers directed the excavation of large trench systems protect-ed from hostile fire. These trenches advanced slowly in a zigzag pattern toward the moat. As the trenches moved forward, batteries of artillery were positioned to return defensive fire and open breaches in the walls. By the time secondary trenches reached the covered walkway, the conclusive assault was under way. Attackers tunneled below the moat to reach the main walls. Bastions were blown up at their bases, and the bombardment intensified until a breach that was large enough to allow the passage of troops was opened.

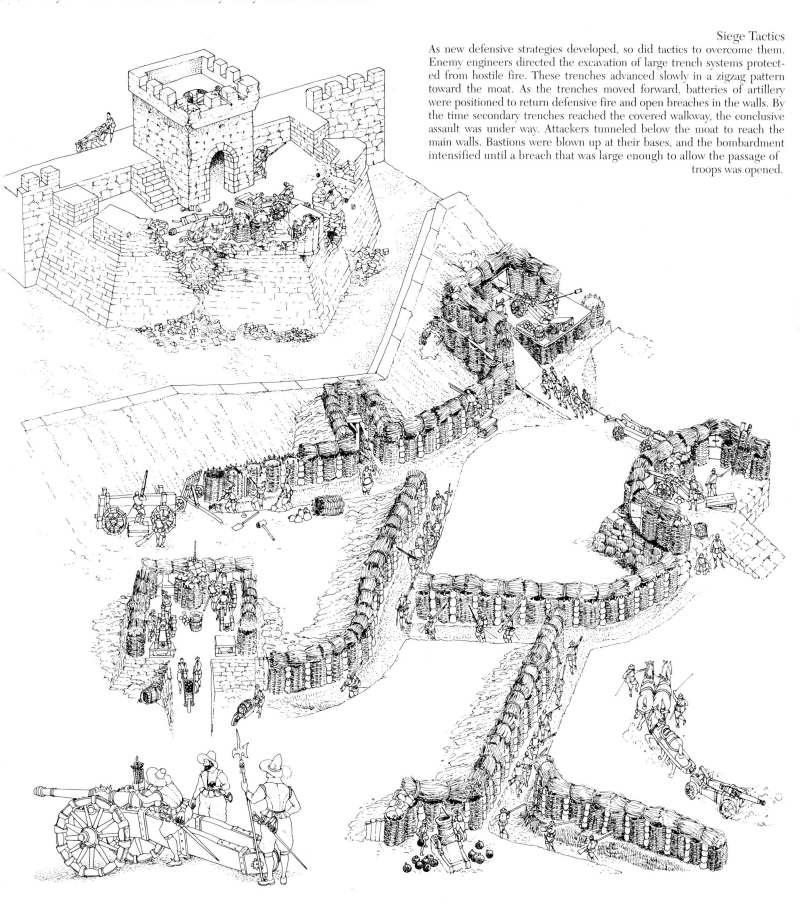

10. FACTORIES AND THE ENLIGHTENMENT: Mid-18th Century

10. FACTORIES AND THE ENLIGHTENMENT
MID-18TH CENTURY

In the mid-eighteenth century Barmi again experienced major so[c]
and economic transformations. A primitive form of capitalism beg[
Larger merchants, no longer willing to buy products at the guilds' h[i]
prices, created their own workshop. In the process, low-paying jo[
were provided to peasants from the rural environs. The first factor[
grew from these buildings specially adapted to produce a single produ[
In contrast to artisans' workshops, they included neither living space [
a sales area. A number of skilled and unskilled workers were employ[
to do specific tasks in exchange for wages. The work was essentially t[
same as before, but mass production enabled the factory owner to s[
his product at a much lower price than the artisan could. Artisans wag[
a fierce struggle to hold their own against the factory system and its p[

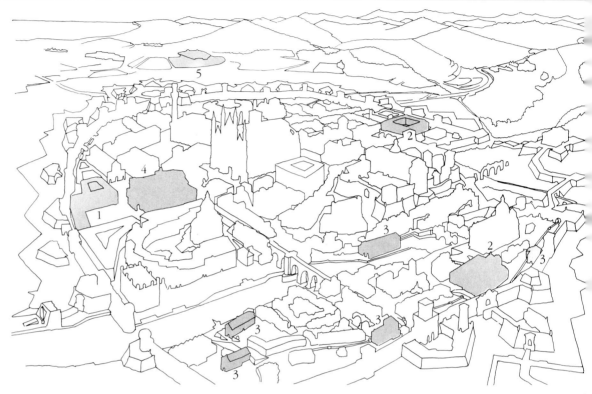

1. Board of trade
Institutions designed to promote economic development grew in power. The board of trade offered merchants and entrepreneurs guidance and support services. To promote economic development and in harmony with the period's spirit of enlightenment, professional and technical courses were offered and scientific research was carried out. In contrast to the university's standard medieval curriculum, the board of trade offered courses that had vital, practical applications.

2. Barracks
At the height of the Enlightenment, barracks designed to accommodate permanent garrisons of royal troops were built. Before this time, soldiers had been quartered in private homes without regard to the wishes of the householders.

3. Factories
Factory buildings were visually unexciting, even though the first ones were designed along neoclassical lines. Inside, laborers worked at specific tasks. Some factories used hydraulic power to drive machinery that facilitated production.

4. Opera
Theater, and above all opera, enjoyed great popularity during this period. These entertainments soon found permanent homes. The opera house, a symbol of both the emerging middle class and the old aristocracy, occupied a position of enormous prestige in the city.

5. Quarantine of the infectious
Epidemics continued to afflict the population. When disease threatened, isolation camps were hastily set up in spots outside the city walls, where ancient hospitals and leper colonies had once stood. When the epidemic passed, these makeshift camps were burned to the ground.

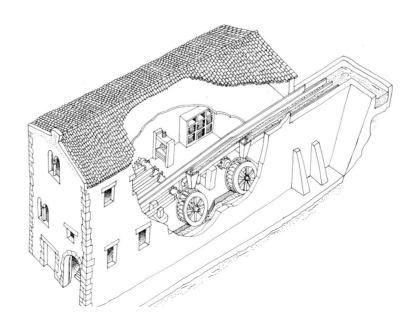

Paper Mill
Cross section of a hydraulic-powered paper mill

Operation of a Paper Mill
The founding in the eighteenth ce[n]tury of the first large factor[ies] coincided with the growing use [of] hydraulic energy to drive machine[ry]. The application of hydraulic pow[er] represented a major technic[al] advance in the textile, ceramic, a[nd] paper industries.
① Cloth rags
② Fulling mill, used to pound rags into pulp
③ Creation of sheets of paper
④ Press
⑤ Drying racks
⑥ Glossing mallet

ters in the new middle class. But the monarchy openly supported the
industrialists, and the artisans and their guilds were eventually wiped
. The industrialists, relieved of their main source of competition,
e free to organize production according to what benefited them.
he factory's rise had a major impact on the urban landscape. As more
l more of these freestanding two-story buildings sprang up, the
and for workers increased. Local peasants and immigrants from
r and far poured into the city, seeking work. Buildings that had for-
rly housed artisans' workshops became workers' lodgings. These
ldings frequently expanded upward to accommodate the burgeoning
an population within limited space.
Barmi's peace was assured during this period by the governance of an

enlightened despot. In the early eighteenth century, Barmi, along with
the entire valley region, had rebelled against the king. The city was
besieged and conquered after a difficult campaign, and the king pun-
ished the Barmians by suspending all their privileges of
self-government. The city was put in the hands of a field marshal, who
strengthened the urban defenses, built barracks, and quartered soldiers.

The king was anxious to exploit the resources of the Barmu region
fully. He encouraged production and trade, and dispatched his military
engineers to design new streets, districts, embankments, and whatever
else was necessary to promote the city's prosperity. The residences and
commercial structures built during this period reflected a taste for neoclassical design.

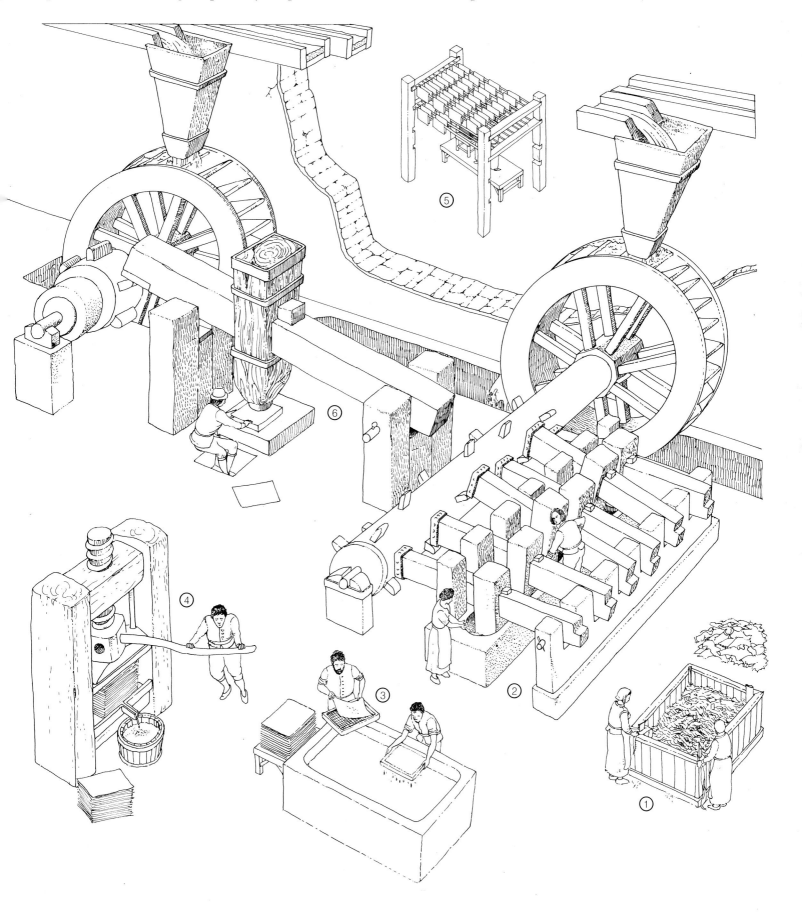

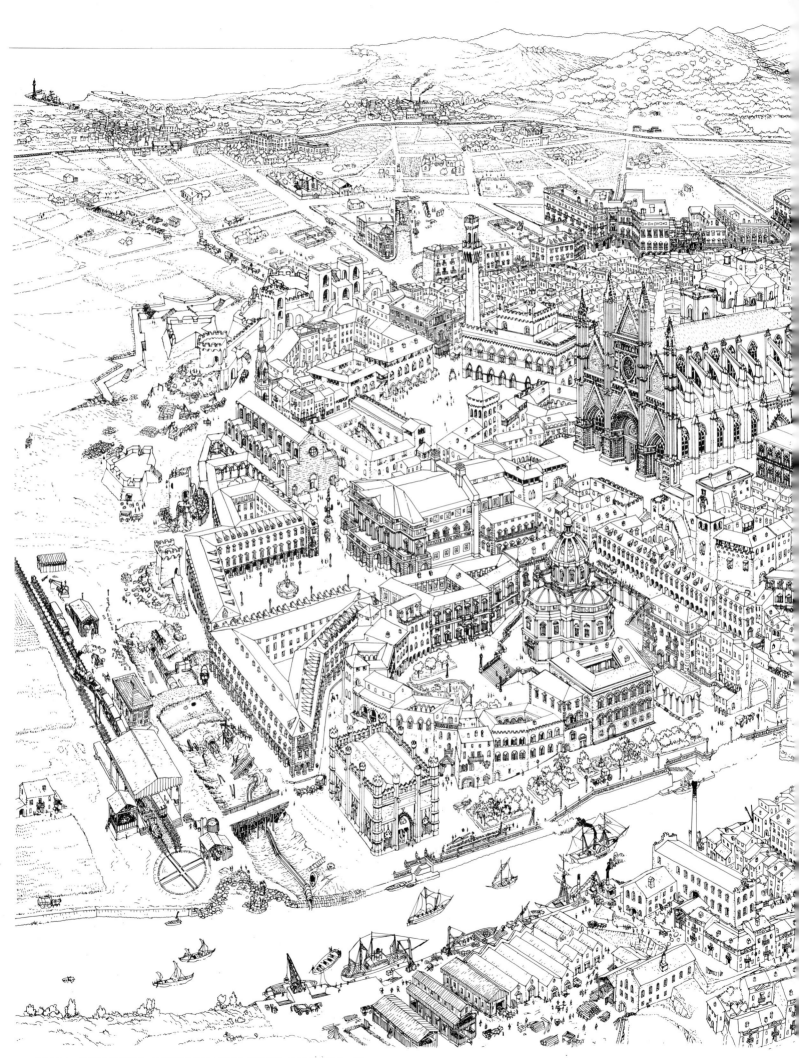

11. OLD STREETS, NEW FACTORIES: Mid-19th Century

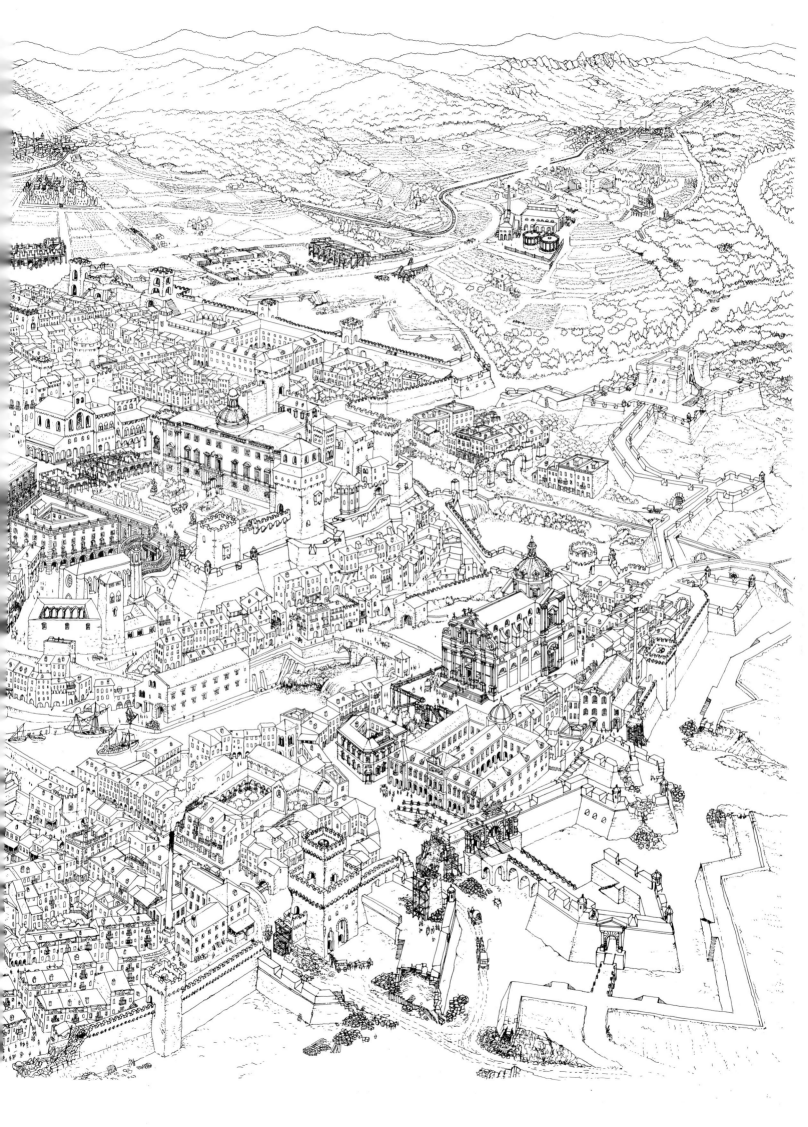

11. OLD STREETS, NEW FACTORIES
MID-19TH CENTURY

Hard-working and prosperous Barmi began to reflect the technolog[...] changes that had already transformed northern Europe and its ind[...] tries. In the 1830s, one factory owner took the financial risk of install[...] a steam engine in his Barmi facility. Steam-powered machinery [...] commonplace in northern Europe by this time, and the installation[...] this first engine began the city's headlong rush toward general mec[...] nization. Although Barmi was only an average-size manufacturing c[...] its skyline soon boasted as many smokestacks as ancient bell towe[...] New factories sprang up within the city center. The river port was ov[...] hauled to facilitate coal deliveries of increasing size and frequency.

The city's working class grew. Hundreds of peasants, drawn away fr[...] the surrounding countryside by the promise of work, arrived in the c[...]

1. Railroad station
The railroad became an integral part of the urban landscape. It served as both a symbol of and a stimulus to nineteenth-century industrialization and progress. Steam locomotives, capable of the astonishing speed of 30 miles per hour, transported people and goods.

2. Steam-powered factories
Such factories first appeared in southern Europe in the 1830s. Their distinctive plants, warehouses, and smokestacks were easily recognizable. Construction and mechanization of most factories followed British models.

3. Gas power plant
Gas illuminated the nineteenth-century city. An underground system carried gas from the power plant to roads, public buildings, homes, and other locations. Its use continued for decades.

4. Working-class districts
The neighborhoods where medieval and Renaissance artisans had operated their workshops be-came crowded, unhealthy quarters for large numbers of laborers. In some of the city's new, undeveloped areas, housing was built for the middle and working classes. The most dis-tinctive characteristic of this housing was its monotonous uniformity.

5. New buildings
The mid-nineteenth century wit-nessed construction of a numb[...] of public buildings previous[...] unknown: bank headquarte[...] specialized schools, a central p[...] office, and a firehouse.

Evolution of an Artisan's House
Over time some artisans' districts evolved into working-class neighborhoods. The old workshops became multistory lodging houses in which laborers and their families lived in cramped, often shared quarters. An auxiliary doorway, cut into the façade, gave access to the common stairway and upper floors.

1640

1780

1850

1910

l sought lodgings. To make room for the new population, former arti-
s' workshops continued to be converted to multistory dwellings. New
ldings also rose to accommodate the laborers. By mid-century, the
's population had grown to 40,000. No room remained for new facto-
s, workers' lodgings, or middle-class homes.
The ramparts that for so long had protected the city now threatened it
h strangulation. The military authorities, however, saw the city wall as
al to their continued control of both the region and Barmi. They
used to tear it down, and they forbade any new buildings at less than
annon shot's distance from the wall. Industrialists who wanted to
ild new factories had to choose sites in surrounding towns.
n spite of the congestion within the city, several important projects to

improve the infrastructure were carried out. The sewer system was
upgraded and extended. A coal-powered plant produced gas to light the
streetlamps. The city council initiated garbage collection and organized
a fire department. Meanwhile, middle-class housing interests competed
with such institutions as the post office and banks for control of the few
remaining building sites.

In the 1840s yet another emblem of industrial progress arrived. A railroad line opened to connect the city to the lower river valley.

In the mid-nineteenth century the central government finally gave in
to Barmian calls for demolition of the ramparts. Within a few years the
wall was dismantled and construction of new suburban districts had
begun. The city was at last free to enjoy unlimited physical expansion.

orking-Class Housing
using for workers and
ir families was built in
tory neighborhoods and
e new industrial suburbs.

Apartment
Bedrooms
Kitchen
Latrine
Well
Cesspool

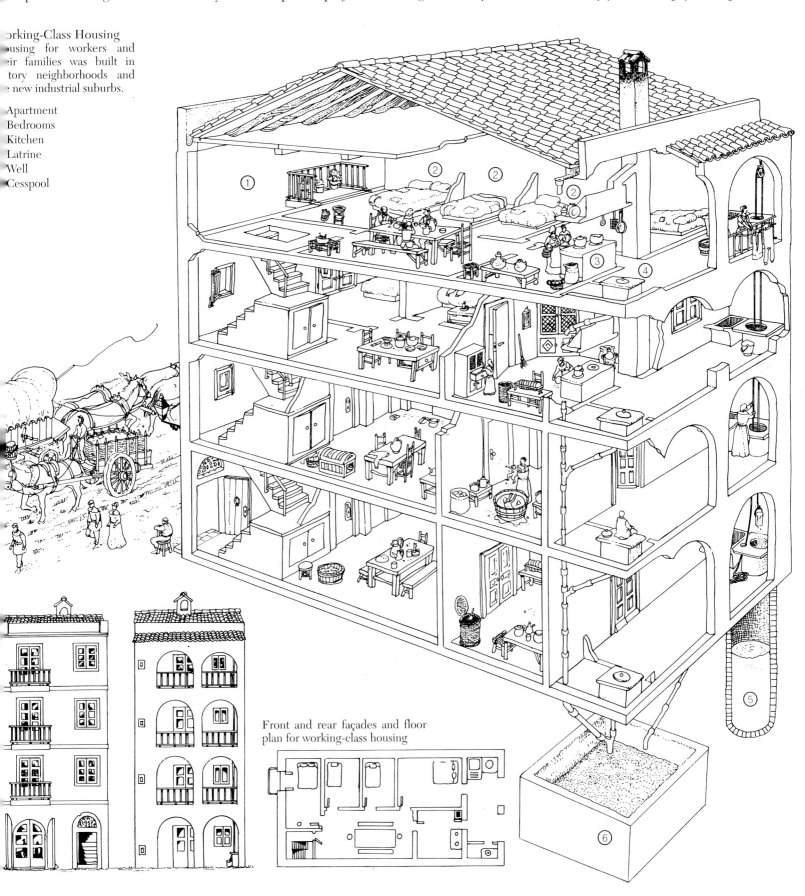

Front and rear façades and floor
plan for working-class housing

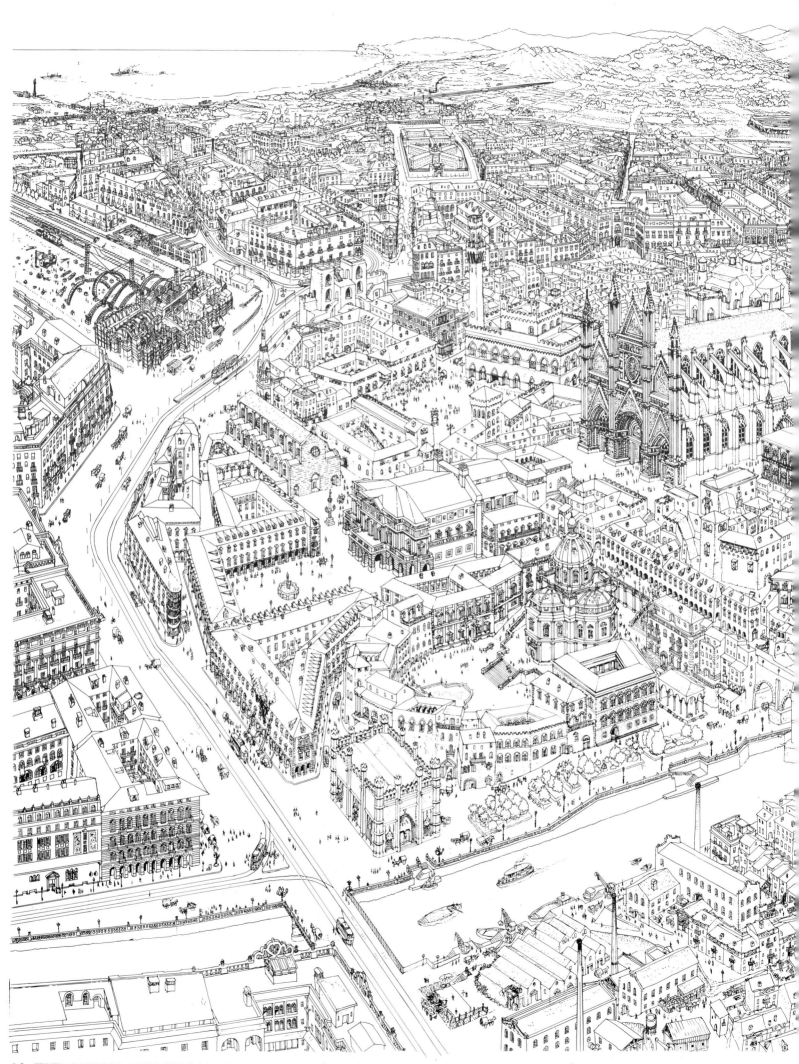

12. EXPANSION AND URBAN GROWTH: Early 20th Century

12. EXPANSION AND URBAN GROWTH
EARLY 20TH CENTURY

During the second half of the nineteenth century, Barmi experien[ced] spectacular growth. Where the ramparts had once stood, broad aven[ues] now ringed the city. Urban development of outlying districts bega[n in] earnest. The city council attempted to direct growth, but with little s[uc]cess. In practice, private initiatives fueled the expansion and specula[tion] drove it.

Spacious residential districts for the middle class quickly sprang [up.] Luxurious residences took their place beside small mansions. Facto[ries] and working-class districts were concentrated in industrial zones.

By the early twentieth century Barmi's population stood at 100,0[00,] and the city had grown to absorb most industrial centers on the s[ur]rounding plain. The urban landscape was radically altered, not onl[y]

1. Central power plant
The increased demand for electricity – in industry, transport, and urban services – prompted construction of major coal-burning plants to produce electricity in quantity.

2. District market
To guarantee ready supplies of groceries and household necessities to the various city districts, the Barmians built large markets that housed stalls and stands of every type. In some markets the bold metal superstructures allowed merchants to build handsome pavilions in which to display their wares.

3. Hospital
The city's growth and its commitment to improved services led to construction of new and modern hospitals. The old medical centers based on medieval models did not meet modern standards of hygiene or of effectiveness.

4. Soccer field
As organized sports events and amateur athletics increased in popularity, the city set aside space for playing fields. By the end of the nineteenth century, enthusiasm for soccer was becoming widespread.

5. New construction
*The city's growth and evolution produced some buildings not pre*viously seen in the urban landscape. These included the editorial offices of daily newspapers, modern jails to replace medieval cells, streetcar garages, movie theaters, a primitive centralized telephone system, banks, and telegraph offices.

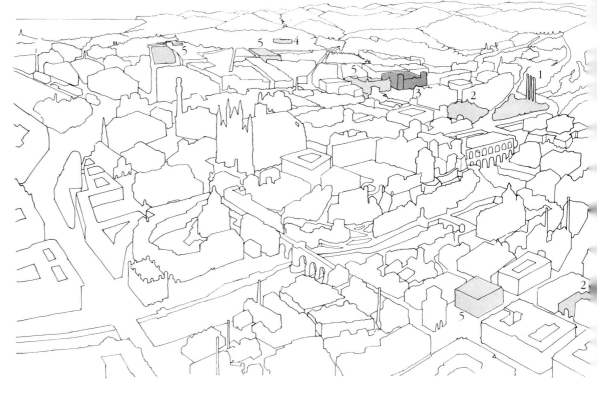

New Residential Plumbing Systems
Newly built houses incorporated modern plumbing systems. Flush toilets and bathtubs were the major innovations of this period.

ect to the vastness of its area but as a result of numerous technologi-
advances. Electric power provided a major stimulus to development.
y factories employed it, and gradually it replaced gas as a source for
ting and transport. Electrical energy powered the streetcar, the most
ular form of transportation during this period. Streetcar lines criss-
ssed the city and streetcar stations dotted the streets.

central electrical plant furnished the city with power. Other new
dings rose to meet the needs and facilitate the functioning of a city
ering the modern industrial age. Streetcar garages were built, as were
ew railroad station, new markets, public schools, museums, and
aries. Standing out from the others because of sheer size were the
university, the medical center, the slaughterhouse, the central mar-

ket, jails, and an enlarged cemetery.

Construction techniques based on the use of reinforced concrete and
structural iron, combined with the aesthetics of art nouveau, Jugendstil,
and modernism, created stunning, bold examples of architectural
design.

Barmi's infrastructure was notably improved. During the phases of
expansion, particular care was taken to ensure the adequacy of the water
and sewage systems. These improvements extended even to the systems
buried beneath the city's historic center.

idential Street
Middle-class apartment building
ewage system
Gas line
Water main
Electric pole
Streetcar
Concrete road surface
Gaslights

13. A MAJOR COMMERCIAL AND INDUSTRIAL CENTER: Mid-20th Century

14. BETWEEN PAST AND FUTURE: Late 20th Century

14. BETWEEN PAST AND FUTURE
LATE 20TH CENTURY

...mi's population has risen dramatically to a new high of 350,000. T... of this growth occurred during the industrialization that follow... War II. Since the beginning of the 1980s, growth has all b... ceased. The urban population has stabilized, and in some districts eve... declined. The concentration of commercial and financial institutions ... the central city has increased, while satellite cities have risen on th... periphery. Industries on the city fringes have moved farther out of tow... The land is being converted into parks and gardens.

Automobile use is now pervasive. Traffic control systems have bee... developed, but traffic jams and illegal parking have become facts... urban life. Use of public transport has declined, and service has wor... ened because of the increased traffic of automobiles. Urban access...

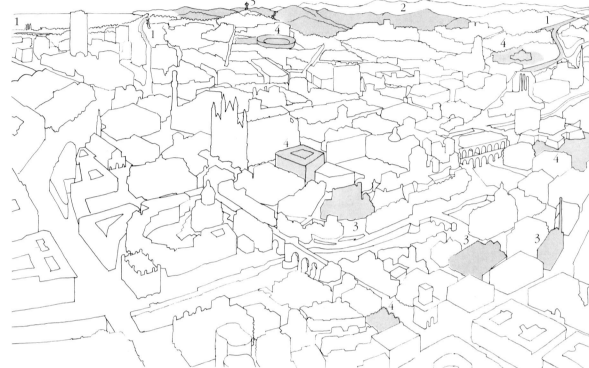

1. Highways and beltways
Increased automobile traffic has created serious access problems in the city. Bypass roads, beltways, and high-speed auto routes are some of the new arteries designed to improve traffic flow.

2. Natural parks
Urban expansion and improved transportation have shortened the distance between the city and the surrounding mountains. The mountains have been declared natural parks, which guarantees urbanites easy access to unspoiled, natural regions.

3. Renovated buildings
Some buildings that have outlived their original function have been restored and converted. They often serve as cultural or entertainment centers.

4. Cultural facilities
Contemporary society's abundance of leisure time has increased the demand for well-maintained sports facilities, concert halls, theaters, museums, and libraries.

5. Telecommunications towers
Telephone, radio, and television systems require enormous towers for transmission of their broadcast signals. The towers' distinctive profiles make them easily recognizable landmarks of the city.

Residential Building
① Elevator
② Underground garage

Street
③ Streetlight
④ Telephone booth
⑤ Traffic light

Underground Infrastructure
⑥ Sewage line
⑦ Water main
⑧ Storm drain
⑨ Gas line
⑩ Telephone lines
⑪ Electrical lines

Subway
⑫ Entrance
⑬ Station
⑭ Tunnels

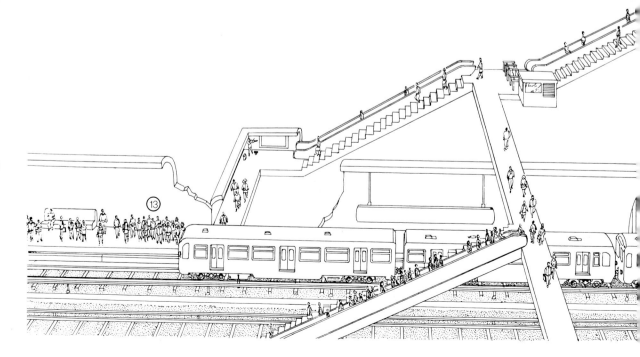

an acute problem. City planners have sought to alleviate the situation by constructing bypasses, connecting highways, and auto routes. Nonetheless, the traffic situation continues to deteriorate. Overcrowding, air and noise pollution, and other problems associated with large urban areas have combined to deprive Barmi of its human scale. Barmi has become an extremely stressful place to live. It has grown too large, and the difficulty of keeping it supplied with power, food, and services is surpassed only by the difficulty of eliminating the mountains of waste it generates.

City authorities are attempting to prevent further deterioration with programs of directed urban growth. Destruction of the city's cultural legacy has been halted by protecting the most significant structures from

construction moratoriums have been placed on many historic sites. With new policies of rehabilitation, urban planners hope to rescue the city's most ancient quarters from decay. Old palaces and early factories have been restored and opened for public view. Equal energy has been given to the creation of parks, sports facilities, and programs aimed at reducing pollution and controlling traffic.

Barmi's present challenge is to restore the human quality to city life. Meeting this challenge means solving the grave problems of overdevelopment created in the latter half of this century. Perhaps the same technology that helped generate the hardships can be used to alleviate them.

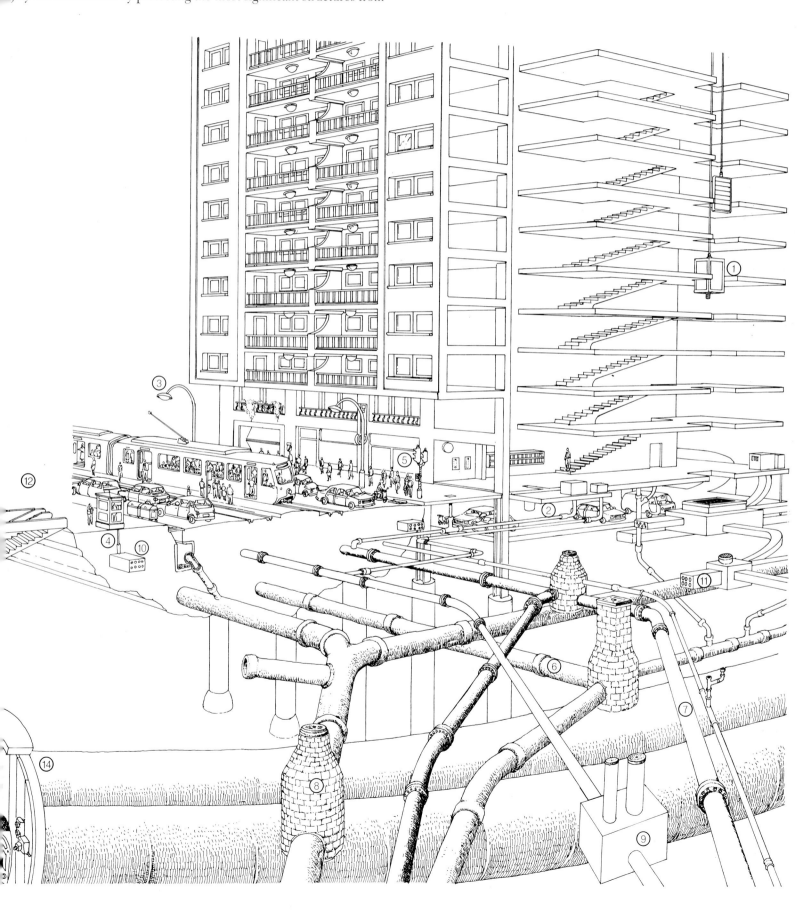

INDEX